The Treasure Hunt Stunt at Fenway Park

The Baseball Geeks Adventures Book 3

David Aretha

THE BASEBALL GEEKS ADVENTURES

The Treasure Hunt Stunt at Fenway Park

The Baseball Geeks Adventures Book 3

David Aretha

Fenway Park™ is a registered trademark and is owned by the Boston Red Sox Baseball Club Limited Partnership. This story has not been authorized by Fenway Park™ or the Boston Red Sox Baseball Club Limited Partnership.

Library of Congress Cataloging-in-Publication Data

Aretha, David.
    The treasure hunt stunt at Fenway Park / David Aretha.
        pages cm.—(The Baseball Geeks adventures ; book 3)
        Summary: "The Baseball Geeks are on their way to Fenway Park to appear on a reality TV show. Joey, Kevin, and Omar are being tested on all of their baseball knowledge, but will they be able to beat the competition and win the Fenway Challenge?"—Provided by publisher.
        ISBN 978-1-62285-128-7
        1. Fenway Park (Boston, Mass.)—Juvenile fiction. 2. Boston Redsox (Baseball team)—Juvenile fiction. [1. Fenway Park (Boston, Mass.)—Fiction. 2. Boston Redsox (Baseball team)—Fiction. 3. Baseball—Fiction. 4. Contests--Fiction.] I. Title.
        PZ7.A6845Tr 2014
        [Fic]—dc23   2012050441

Future editions:
Paperback ISBN: 978-1-62285-129-4   Single-User PDF ISBN: 978-1-62285-132-4
EPUB ISBN: 978-1-62285-131-7   Multi-User PDF ISBN: 978-1-62285-169-0

Printed in the United States of America
072014 HF Group, North Manchester, IN
10 9 8 7 6 5 4 3 2 1

Speeding Star
Box 398, 40 Industrial Road
Berkeley Heights, NJ 07922
USA
www.speedingstar.com

Cover Illustration: © Ingvard the Terrible

CONTENTS

Chapter 1

KEVIN PEES HIS PANTS

"That's the limousine?" I said. "It looks like a stinkin' minivan!"

"Whoa!" my dad shot back. "Who do you think you are—Snooki Polizzi? Keep your ego in check, Joe. You're no TV star."

As we boarded the "limousine" on a sparkling May day at Boston's Logan Airport, Kevin and Omar were cracking up.

"Snooki Polizzi . . . ," Kevin said through his giggles.

"He could have said Mike 'the Situation,'" added Omar, flailing his long arms for emphasis. "But instead he called you Snooki!"

"Ha ha ha—we're all laughing," I replied.

Weeks earlier, Omar, Kevin, and I—known around our suburban-Cleveland school as the "Baseball Geeks"—were asked to appear on a reality TV show called *Sports Jr.* The producers were looking for four groups of famous "baseball kids" to appear in their "Fenway Challenge," which would involve riddles and a treasure hunt. They chose us as one of the four groups. Us Geeks had become nationally famous due to our involvement with the "Curse of Omar" and the Chicago Cubs. (It's a long story. You'll have to read about it in *Foul Ball Frame-up at Wrigley Field.*)

Anyway, there aren't too many famous baseball kids, so it was like they *had* to pick us.

The six of us climbed into the "limo," with Omar, Kevin, and I sharing the last row. Omar, who has a huge collection of MLB caps, wore his newly bought Red Sox cap for this special weekend. The "dads" sat in front of us, and what a threesome *they* were! My dad, Matthew Evers, is a clean-cut airplane mechanic who used to serve in the National Guard. Almost a year ago, he had to move two hundred miles away to Dayton, Ohio, to find work. So this was a rare chance for me to spend time with him.

Mr. Kernacki, Kevin's dad, has spent time in jail and in a mental hospital. But that was years ago. He's working now, and he's a nice guy. He's also distinctive-looking, with curly, golden hair; a mustache; and circle frame glasses. Then there's Mr. Ovozi, Omar's dad. He's a tall, thin, dark-haired man from Uzbekistan. He speaks with an accent and talks loudly, especially when he says, "Ohhh-marrr!"

As for Omar, who is half Uzbek and half African American, he was downloading the free "Bah-ston Accent" app on his dad's smartphone. Kevin and I were already laughing.

"Okay," said Omar, "it says that you first need to know the Boston vocabulary. A person from South Boston is called a Southie. And instead of eating a sub sandwich, you chow down on a grinder—also called a spuckie."

"Would Snooki eat a spuckie?" quipped Kevin, who still had a case of the giggles.

"Snooki's from New Jersey," Mr. Ovozi bellowed.

Kev was doubling over in laughter. Normally, he's a serious, often-nervous kid. But I think he—like Omar and I— was just excited to be on this adventure.

"Okay," Omar announced, as we drove through Ted Williams Tunnel. "What's a Chowda Head?"

"Shhh!" I said, pointing to the driver.

"Nah, it's not an insult," he said. "It just means someone from Boston. Like if you live in Wisconsin, you're a Cheesehead."

"What if you're from Ohio?" I asked.

"Dad," Omar said. "What is Ohio known for?"

"Making rubber tires," he replied.

"Rubberheads!" Kevin squeaked while clutching his tummy in laughter.

Mr. Kernacki turned around, smiling. "Kevin," he said. "Don't pee your pants."

That got Omar and I cracking up.

"Hey, Joe," Omar asked me while reading about Boston accents. "Ask the dri-vah . . . if he can drive the cah . . . to Mah-tha's Vin-yahd . . . so we can have lobstah . . . for suppa!"

All three dads turned around, looking at Omar—or should I say, O-mah—with amused expressions. As for Kevin, he was now double-clutching his stomach, he was laughing so hard. A tear rolled out of the corner of his eye. Then he put his hands over his lap.

"Wait," I said to him. "You didn't . . ."

"A little bit!" he said.

"Oh, brother," Mr. Kernacki said, shaking his head and smiling. "When the cameras are rolling, Kev, make sure you hold it in."

Kevin was able to change his pants in style. That's because the *Sports Jr.* producers set us up in the Boston Marriott Long Wharf hotel. It has spectacular views of the Boston Harbor, with all its sailboats and yachts. The lobby was modern and massive, and the rooms had massive flat-screen TVs in high-def.

That night, Kevin suggested we walk to the water and watch the sun set on the Atlantic Ocean. The five of us had to remind him that the sun *rises* in the East and sets in the West. "Oh, yeah," he said. We ended up walking the streets of Boston looking for some grub. We thought that Yankee Lobster was an odd name for a restaurant, since Bostonians hate the New York Yankees. We wound up at a sandwich shop that named its "grindas" and other meals after famous Red Sox players.

Omar got the "Big Papi," a ginormous burger that honored All-Star slugger David "Big Papi" Ortiz. Kevin ordered the "Gooey Dewey," a cheesy sandwich named after legendary right fielder Dwight "Dewey" Evans. And I got "the Splendid Splinter," which came with .406 pounds of corned beef. As everyone in Boston knows, Ted "the Splendid Splinter" Williams batted .406 one year for the Red Sox.

But the real fun began the next morning, when we cabbed it to Fenway Park™. En route to the ballpark, we strolled past Red Sox memorabilia shops, eateries, and old-fashioned light poles.

"I always thought of Fenway Park as being all green," my dad said. "But the exterior is largely red brick."

Hanging down from the brick walls were enormous banners. Each one signified a Red Sox championship, be it an Eastern Division title (white banner), American League title (blue), or World Series championship (red).

"How come," Mr. Ovozi asked, "there are no red banners between 1918 and 2004?"

Omar, Kev, and I explained. The Red Sox went eighty-six years without winning a World Series. Many people blamed it on the "Curse of the Bambino," meaning Babe Ruth. After Fenway Park opened in 1912, the Red Sox won four World Series through 1918, including three with Ruth. But Boston traded that great pitcher-turned-slugger to the

Yankees after the 1919 season. From 1920 to 2003, the Yankees won 26 World Series titles and the Red Sox won zero!

The Red Sox came oh-so-close many times. In 1946, 1967, 1975, and 1986, they made it to Game 7 of the World Series—and lost. In 1946, it was "Slaughter's Mad Dash" that did them in. In 1967, Boston's "Impossible Dream" season came up one win short. Catcher Carlton Fisk won Game 6 of the '75 Series with a thrilling twelfth-inning home run, but the BoSox lost Game 7 to Cincinnati's "Big Red Machine." The 1986 title seemed in the bag . . . until the Sox blew a two-run, tenth-inning, Game 6 lead to the New York Mets.

The Red Sox faithful are known as the most devoted and knowledgeable fans in baseball. Eighty-six years of losing took its toll on them. Diehard fans lived long lives and never saw their team win a World Series.

"Until 2004," Kevin said. "They were down three games to none to the Yankees in the American League Championship Series, and then won four straight."

"They reversed 'The Curse,'" Omar said.

"And then they swept St. Louis in the World Series," I added.

"If you know all that about the Red Sox," Mr. Ovozi said, "then I think you are ready for the Fenway Challenge."

"Yeah, maybe," replied Omar. "Unless their questions are . . . hah-da."

Chapter 2

GEARING UP FOR THE FENWAY CHALLENGE

Like baseball legends of yore, Kevin, Omar, and I stood in the outfield of Fenway Park.

"Babe Ruth roamed this grass," Kevin marveled. "And Joe DiMaggio and Ty Cobb and Mickey Mantle."

"And Coco Crisp," Omar added.

Kevin and I grimaced.

"He used to play for the Sox," Omar explained. "It's one of my favorite all-time baseball names, along with

Wonderful Terrific Monds, Ed Head, and Pickles Dilhoeffer."

In an empty Fenway Park on a sunny Saturday morning, we were about to be prepped for the Fenway Challenge. The *Sports Jr.* crew consisted of a producer, a director, a sound guy, two camera operators, and the show's host: Skip Waybak. We worked mostly with the director, Bernie Rohrbacher, an older guy with a big belly and a bushy, scraggly beard. He was the complete opposite of Skip, a handsome, energetic young man with thick black hair and a blinding smile.

"I'm a Yankees fan," Mr. Rohrbacher announced with a chuckle, "so let's get this over with. We're going to begin filming in the Green Monster seats."

Uh-oh, I thought. *I'm scared of heights, and the Green Monster seats are like the top of Jack's beanstalk.* The Green Monster in left field is the most famous wall in baseball. It rises thirty-seven feet high. At the base of the Monster is a manually operated scoreboard. Red Sox stadium workers enter the scoreboard room from the outfield through a door that's in the wall. When a team scores a run, someone inside the room changes the number for fans to see.

Hitters have a love-hate relationship with the Monster. It's only 315 feet down the left-field line, so a towering fly ball can easily sail over it. On the other hand, a screaming line drive—which would be a homer in every other ballpark—will bang off the wall, resulting in a double or maybe even a single.

Anyway, a few years back, they built 274 seats above the Green Monster. And that's where we were headed.

"Ya know," Mr. Rohrbacher joked. "We could take the ladder."

A ladder rises to the top of the Monster. Years ago, there used to be a large net behind the wall to prevent home run balls from damaging storefronts on Lansdowne Street. Stadium workers would climb the ladder to retrieve the balls from the netting. Luckily, climbing the ladder wasn't part of the Fenway Challenge. We hopped into the stands and walked up to the Monster seats. Our dads came with us, but they had to sit off on the side.

As we sat high above Fenway Park, we got to meet the other contestants. One "group" was a pair of nine-year-old sisters, the Fernandez Twins. They traveled to ballparks all over the country, singing the national anthem and "God Bless America."

"If we can't beat these kindergartners in a baseball challenge," Kevin said, "we might as well pack up and go home."

"They're not in *kindergarten*, Kevin," I said.

The two Kansas City Kids looked like tougher competition. One day last summer, they happened to be sitting in a near-empty section behind the left-field fence at Kauffman Stadium. In that game, the Royals and Detroit Tigers belted six home runs.

These two kids, a couple of happy-go-lucky junior high buddies, caught *four* of those home run balls.

According to the Society for American Baseball Research, they almost certainly set an MLB record for home runs caught by friends in a game. The two kids introduced themselves to us and shook our hands. They were nice guys.

The same could not be said for the remaining group. Muscles, Star, and the Lip is what Kevin called the three star players from the reigning Little League World Series championship team.

I'm sure they were nice kids—yada, yada, yada—but they were mean to us. Muscles was tall and athletic and already forming muscles. Star had long blond hair that he frequently flicked back with his hand, like a movie star. And the Lip curled his upper lip into a mean-looking sneer.

"So let me get this straight," Star told Omar as we climbed up to the Green Monster seats. "We're here because we're the best Little League players in the entire world. And you're here because you dropped a Coke on a Cubs outfielder's head."

His teammates laughed.

"I think it was a Pepsi," Muscles inserted.

"Oh," said the Lip. "Excuuuuuuuuse me!"

They laughed again, while Omar took their insults in silence.

"Don't let 'em get to you, Big O," Kevin told Omar. "They're trying to intimidate you—get in your head."

"They think they're so great," I said, "but they're really low-class."

Still, you don't become Little League champions unless you're extremely disciplined and highly knowledgeable about baseball. In the Fenway Challenge, I predicted, they would be our toughest competition.

We soon settled in to our sky-high Monster seats. I was all right until I looked down on the field, which sent a shiver up my legs. To make us kids feel at ease before filming, Skip cracked a couple corny jokes.

"Why did they stop selling bottled soda at the doubleheader?" Skip asked.

Why?

"Because the home team lost the opener," he said.

Groan.

Skip continued: "A doctor is talking to his patient. The doc says, 'I got good news and bad news. The good news is that they play baseball in heaven.' The patient says, 'What's the bad news?' The doctor says, 'The bad news is that you're pitching on Wednesday.'"

That was pretty funny. Then, with the cameras rolling, Skip explained our mission. He took on a very serious tone, as if we were CIA agents or something. I could imagine dramatic music in the background once this was on TV.

"Your mission, boys . . . and girls . . . is to answer four Fenway-related riddles during today's Orioles–Red Sox game. The first two groups to prevail in the Riddle Round will advance to the Treasure Hunt Round. And the team that prevails in *that* round will have a chance—not a guarantee, but a chance—to win the Fenway Challenge grand prize."

"What's the grand prize?" Omar asked.

"It's the stuff of legends, Omar," Skip said. "A fantasy come true."

Skip paused for dramatic effect, and the cameras panned our faces. I was very curious about the grand prize, but Skip would not reveal what it was. After he spoke, they turned off the cameras and concession workers came by with bags of food. We each got a Fenway

Frank—a hot dog with relish and chopped onions—along with fries and a cola. My mom, who works at the Vega-Vita health food store, would not have been pleased.

Kevin, meanwhile, barely touched his food. He started rubbing an upper tooth, making a squeaky sound, which he does whenever he gets nervous. The pressure of the Fenway Challenge was getting to him, even before it began.

"A camera is gonna follow us the whole time, Joe," Kevin said. "What if we can't answer any of the riddles? The whole country will think we're a trio of morons."

"I thought you *wanted* to do this," I said.

"It *sounded* like fun," he said, "but now we actually have to *do* it."

By noon, the Red Sox began to take the field and fans started to fill the seats. I, too, started feeling anxious. Before the national anthem, Skip gathered all four groups of kids together in the right-field seating area.

"I forgot to mention," he told all of us while the cameras were filming. "Before you can even begin the Riddle Round, you must befriend the enemies."

He said it again, with stronger emphasis: "*Befriend* the enemies."

"What the heck does that mean?" the Lip asked (except he didn't say "heck").

"You have to figure it out," Skip said with a fiendish smile.

"The Star-Spangled Banner" began, which meant that everyone had to stand to attention. Kevin struggled for breath—he was really getting nervous.

When the anthem ended, amid roaring applause, we got down to work.

"All right, befriend the enemies," I said. "Who's the enemy?"

I looked to my left and saw a camera in my face. This was going to be very strange. We didn't even have our dads around for support; they were watching the game—and us—from a skybox.

Just then, the Fernandez Twins approached us. They both were wearing white dresses, which I thought was an odd choice for a ballpark challenge. One of them tapped me on the shoulder

"Excuse me," she said. "But I think we're supposed to befriend you."

Kevin huffed. My fear that he was going to be snotty to the girls was realized.

"No, no, no," he told the girl. "Why don't you run along and play now, okay?"

"Uh, guys," Omar said while pointing his long arm toward the third base seating area. "Look over there."

The Little League Champs were talking to a young woman in a Cardinals jacket.

"The Cardinals are an enemy!" I blurted. "An enemy of the Red Sox, 'cause they beat 'em in the '46 and '67 World Series."

With the Fernandez girls following us, we looked around the ballpark for more people in Cardinals jackets.

As we walked down a crowded aisle toward right field, a curious peanut vendor stopped us.

"Whatcha kids lookin' fo-ah?" he asked in his local accent.

We explained about the show and "befriending the enemy."

"Well, I don't see no Cahdinals jackets," the vendor said, "but I see guys in Rays and White Sox jackets. And they're lookin' at ya."

Cardinals, Rays, and White Sox.

"Those are all teams that beat Boston in the postseason," Kevin explained. "Hence, 'the enemy!'"

"And I see Mets and Yankees jackets, too," added a Fernandez twin.

These girls were more baseball savvy than I had thought. The Mets had beaten the Sox in the '86 World Series, and the Yankees had knocked them out in the 2003 American League Championship Series, when Aaron Boone belted an extra-inning, walk-off homer in Game 7.

"That was a haht-breakah!" the vendor recalled.

The Fernandez girls ran to the man in the Rays jacket, and we hoofed it to the woman in the Yankees garb. She was a short woman in her fifties or sixties, with big earrings and poofy bleached-blonde hair. We would find out later that she was the director's wife. We introduced ourselves, and she was really nice.

"You're all so handsome!" she said. "I'm Laverne, and I'm from Brooklyn. And though I hate the Red Sox, I'm gonna help you kids win."

Kevin was feeling better already.

"I'm gonna take you through the Riddle Round," she said. "I got all four questions, and they're really hard. I am authorized to help you—but only to a certain extent. So you all got to use your noodles."

She tapped my head.

"So, are you ready?" she asked.

"We're ready!" I replied.

The Fenway Challenge was about to begin.

Chapter 3

ROARING THROUGH THE RIDDLE ROUND

Standing in an aisle in the right-field area, squinting from the afternoon sun, us Geeks were ready to answer our first riddle. But Laverne wasn't.

"So, Omar, what nationality are you?" she asked.

"I'm African American and Uzbek," he said.

"Oh, that's interesting! I have a cousin, Carl, who married an Uzbek woman. She was gorgeous, but she wore too much makeup, in my opinion. Or 'IMO.' Right? 'In My Opinion'?"

Kevin was really getting antsy. I could read his mind: *We're on the clock here, lady! Let's get the show on the road!*

Laverne pulled a piece of paper out of the pocket of her Yankees jacket.

"All right, your first riddle," she said.

She looked down and read.

"Sunk before it began," she said.

Kevin contorted his face.

"Huh?" he said. "What does that have to do with baseball?"

"It's the Fenway Challenge," was Laverne's vague response.

"So . . . we don't get any clues?" Omar asked.

"You have to think it through," she said. "That's life. Things are not handed to us on a silver platter—unless your last name is Kardashian."

"Well, what sinks?" I asked.

"Boats," Omar said. "But a boat has nothing to do with baseball. Can a ball itself sink—like in a puddle during a game?"

"Baseballs float," said Kevin, who was getting frustrated. "This is just too hard."

"Oh, I know!" I said. "Maybe Fenway Park sank before it was opened—you know, back in 1912."

Kevin gave me a funny face.

"How can a baseball stadium sink?" he blurted. "What did they do: build it in the Boston Harbor?"

"The Bah-ston Hah-ba," Omar quipped.

"Well, maybe something else sank before the ballpark opened," I said.

"Now you're talkin'!" exclaimed Laverne.

That's how, it seemed, she was going to help us. Whenever we got close to an answer, she would blurt out, "Now you're talkin'!" I wished instead that she had a computer we could Google on. But at least now we were close. Something sank before Fenway Park opened.

"It's got to be a boat," Omar said. "But what boats do we know that sank? . . . Kev?"

"What are you looking at me for?" Kevin asked. "Am I the expert on leaky boats? The only boat with a hole in it that I know of was the one in that movie."

"The *Titanic*?" Omar asked.

Wait. The *Titanic* sank a long time ago, and Fenway opened in 1912. Laverne couldn't suppress a smile.

"It's got to be the *Titanic*!" I said. "It probably sank a few years before Fenway Park opened."

"So that's your answer?" Laverne asked.

Kevin and I nodded.

"Okay," Omar said. "The *Titanic* sank before Fenway began."

"You got it!" Laverne exclaimed, jumping up and down.

"All right!" I said, slapping high-fives with Kev and the Big O.

"And you know what?" she added. "It actually sank on April 15, 1912, just *two days* before the Red Sox were scheduled to play their first-ever game at Fenway. In fact, it put a damper on the grand-opening festivities. Everyone felt horrible about that the disaster. Fifteen hundred people died, you know. . . . But, life goes on."

We were quickly distracted by a long fly ball to right field. The crowd rose to its feet and roared mightily as a David

Ortiz blast landed over the fence. Kevin's eyes grew big.

"Holy cannoli, look who caught the ball!" Kevin exclaimed.

While talking with a guide, one of the Kansas City Kids had grabbed it with his bare hands. Now he was smiling and showing it off to the happy fans.

"Man, home runs just fall into those guys' hands," Kevin said, still in disbelief.

Anyway, it was back to business. Next riddle.

"Christened by president's blood," Laverne read. "And you have to explain the meaning."

Again, Kevin twisted his face. He threw up his hands as if to say, "Heh?" Stan the cameraman, through his fuzzy red beard, smiled. With all of his antics, Kev was making for "good TV." Maybe he would be the next Honey Boo Boo!

As for the riddle, the guys and I chewed on it for five minutes and were getting nowhere. We weren't even sure what "christened" meant, except that people christen a new building by smashing a bottle of champagne on it. So maybe the president in 1912 did so on Fenway Park and cut himself. But we didn't know who the president was that year.

"Come with me," Laverne said.

"Where are we going?" I asked.

"The place with all the answers: the library," she said.

"Fenway Park has a library?" Omar asked.

Kevin shook his head. "Yeah, Omar, they tore down all the skyboxes and replaced them with the world's largest reference section."

"You're a feisty little one!" Laverne said to Kev. "There's actually a cab waiting for us outside. The driver can take us to wherever we need to go. In this case, a presidential library might be a good idea."

The cameraman followed us toward the exit. Just our luck, we passed the Little League snots.

"Where are *you* going?" Muscles asked.

We explained.

"You have to go to the *library* to figure that out!" Muscles shot back. "That question is *so* easy."

Man, those kids were aggravating.

"Wait," I asked Laverne. "Aren't we going to lose a lot of time and fall behind if we have to go to this library?"

"Each of the groups are going on a field trip," Laverne said. "The Little

League Champs will be descending into Boston's sewer system. Which is good, 'cause they could use a little humility."

Forty minutes later, we arrived at the John F. Kennedy Presidential Library and Museum. It was as impressive as Fenway Park. Part of the complex was a 125-foot-high white tower that pointed toward the sky. Another part included a huge wall of dark glass. The complex was built right on the water, probably because President Kennedy had served in the Navy and loved to sail.

The Kennedy Museum was totally cool. My favorite exhibit was the Oval Office, which recreated JFK's White House office when he was president in the early 1960s. It included replicas of his carpeting, drapes, and furniture, as well as the rocking chair he used for his bad back.

"Have a seat," the tour guide said to us, pointing to the desk.

We were stunned.

"We can sit at the desk?" I asked.

"Sure," the guide said. "It's not an authentic chair."

"Omar," Laverne said excitedly, "you can be our first African-Uzbek-American president!"

Omar, who enjoyed hamming things up, sat at President Kennedy's desk. A college-age male intern, who accompanied the tour guide, handed Omar a piece of paper.

"Here, you can read this into the camera," the intern told Omar.

Stan the cameraman focused straight on Omar's face. The Big O cleared his throat. He stretched out his lanky arms and wiggled his fingers.

"Is the camwa on?" Omar asked, imitating Kennedy's Boston accent. We were all giggling by this point. Omar got real serious. He looked hard into the camera.

"And so, my feller Americans," he declared. "Ask not what yer country can do fer you. Ask what you can do fer ya country."

We cracked up, but Omar wasn't finished. He pounded hard on the desk—making the tour guide cringe—and declared loudly: "My feller citizens of the wor-ahd: Ask not what America will do fer you, but what togetha we can do fer the freedom of man!"

We erupted in cheers, including the cameraman.

"Now *that's* good TV!" Stan beamed.

Unfortunately, we were wasting precious time. The tour guide took us to the JFK Library, where light poured in through windows in the ceiling high above. We met a reference librarian, who pulled *History of the Presidents* off a shelf for us. Remember, the riddle was "Christened by president's blood." We discovered that William Howard Taft was the president in April 1912, when Fenway Park opened. The book *Baseball and the Presidents* stated that Taft was a huge baseball fan. He attended fourteen major-league games as president. However, *none* were at Fenway Park.

So, christened by a president's blood? We were still clueless.

"At this point," Laverne said, "I am authorized to give you a hint. What's President Kennedy's full name?"

"John F. Kennedy," Kevin said.

"John *Fitzgerald* Kennedy," I corrected.

"Ah-ha!" beamed Laverne. "And who christened Fenway Park?"

That required more research. In the bowels of the JFK Library, we found a book on the history of Fenway. In 1912, we read, Boston Mayor John Fitzgerald threw out the ceremonial first pitch at the first game at Fenway Park. He thus "christened" it.

"But how does that relate to the president's blood?" I asked.

A light bulb went off in Kevin's head.

"Fitzgerald!" he exclaimed. "Mayor Fitzgerald was probably a *blood relative* of John Fitzgerald Kennedy!"

"Bingo!" Laverne said. "I'll put that down as a correct answer!"

The librarian explained to us that Mayor Fitzgerald was actually John F. Kennedy's mother's father. So JFK's grandfather actually threw out the very first ceremonial pitch at Fenway Park.

"It's a small world," Laverne said. "It's like the time I bumped into my Aunt Loretta in a bakery in Warsaw, Poland."

Anyway, we cabbed it back to Fenway Park lickety-split. At the time we arrived, a U.S. Marine was singing "God Bless America" during the Seventh Inning Stretch. The Red Sox were routing Baltimore 7–1, and the Little League Champs were lounging in box seats eating funnel cakes and cotton candy. They had completed their riddles and had advanced to the Treasure Hunt Round. The Fernandez Twins and the Kansas City Kids were still dealing with riddles, meaning we still had a chance.

"But we better kick butt *now*," Kevin said, as we huddled near the Fenway Favorites food stand.

Laverne read the next riddle.

"The critter," she said, dramatically, "helped *us* watch *him* wave it."

We looked at Laverne with blank faces. Whenever she first read a riddle, it just seemed impossible. We did figure out what "him wave it" meant. It referred to Carlton Fisk belting his twelfth-inning home run in Game 6 of the 1975 World Series. Fisk skied the ball down the left-field line. It had the distance for a home run, but would it be fair or foul? The NBC-TV audience watched as Fisk flung his arms to the right several times, trying to "wave" it fair. It became one of the most famous images in baseball history. The ball clanged off the yellow pole for a home run.

"So we did 'watch him wave it,'" Omar said.

Now we just had to figure out "the critter."

"This is a hard one," Laverne said. "I'm going to let you kids figure out 'the critter' by asking fans at the ballpark."

"*Any* fans?" Kevin asked.

Any fans, Laverne said. I was feeling confident. Bostonians know their Red Sox history like theologians understand the Bible. We approached a slender man with graying hair who donned a Red Sox windbreaker and cap. He was happy to help us out—and he immediately knew the answer.

"You know what goes on inside that Green Monster?" the man asked.

"Yeah, that's where they operate the scoreboard," I replied.

"Yes," he said, "but in the 1975 World Series, NBC had a cameraman in there. Back then, the Green Monster room was nasty—dark and dirty and infested with rats. When Fisk came to bat, the cameraman intended to follow the path of the ball if it were hit toward him. That is what the NBC director had instructed him to do."

"But when Fisk hit the ball," the man continued, "the guy noticed that a rat had jumped on his camera. The guy was freaked. Instead of swiveling the camera to follow the ball, he kept his camera focused on Fisk. So we all got to see that wonderful, magical moment of Carlton Fisk 'waving' the ball fair."

"So when I say, 'The critter helped us watch him wave it,'" Laverne said, "the critter is . . . ?"

"The rat!" we said.

"You got it!" Laverne cried.

We thanked the man repeatedly, then focused hard on the next question. If we answered it correctly—and quickly— we'd make it to the Treasure Hunt Round. The Kansas City Kids were scratching their heads in the right-field bleachers. The Fernandez Twins were nowhere to be found; they were probably still on their field trip.

"Come on, let's nail this one!" Kevin said.

Before the final riddle, a stadium worker handed us three cups of Coke, with the Coca-Cola logo on the cups. I found out later that the Coke company had paid for us to drink their soda on camera. How much they paid, I don't know. But it sure quenched our thirst as the sun beat down on us.

Laverne read the last riddle. Her eyes grew big. Her expression was sinister.

"The seat," she said, "of *horrors.*"

Dang, I thought. *Another hard one.*

"It's got to be a seat in Fenway in which somebody died," I said.

"Or maybe a lot of people died in it," Omar said.

"What do you mean, a lot of people?" Kevin asked, quizzically.

"You know," Omar said. "Don't sit in Seat 22—you're gonna have a haht attack!"

The Big O pretended to have a heart attack, putting his hand over his chest and sticking his tongue out. Good TV.

"Or maybe the seat is haunted," I added. "I heard that ghosts are within these walls."

"Well, I'll tell you this," Laverne said. "The seat is not haunted and nobody died in it."

Still, we were stumped. Didn't have a clue. Laverne led us on a walk, toward the seats near the Red Sox dugout. By this point, it was the top of the ninth inning of an 8–1 game and the fans were starting to leave.

"Take a load off," Laverne said, and we sat down on three empty seats.

"Joe," she said. "You are now sitting in the seat of horrors."

I immediately jumped up and looked down at the seat, while Kevin and Omar cracked up.

"Don't worry!" Laverne laughed. "It's not gonna gobble you up."

"You know," Omar said, "horrors doesn't have to be something real-life horrible. It could be like a horror movie."

"Now you're talkin'!" Laverne said. "A horror movie or a horror . . ."

"A play?" I said. "Or a book?"

"Ding-ding-ding-ding-ding-ding!" Laverne chimed.

"A horror story centered around this seat?" Kevin said.

Laverne shook her head no.

"A horror writer . . . uh . . ." Omar stammered.

Laverne nodded frantically.

"A horror writer sat here," Kevin said.

"Yes!" Laverne exclaimed, throwing up her arms as if we had just scored a touchdown.

"A famous horror writer?" I asked.

"Yes," Laverne responded. "The king of horror writers. Oops!"

The fans sitting around us were laughing. They all knew the answer. And now I did, too. It was the famous author who used to attend all the Red Sox games. He probably had season tickets for this particular seat.

"Stephen King," I said.

"You got it, hun!" Laverne said, giving me a hug.

"Way to come through in the clutch, Super Joe!" Kevin exclaimed.

Skip Waybak came running down the steps, microphone in hand, to greet us.

"Guess who's going to the Treasure Hunt Round!" Skip effused.

"Woo-hoo!" cheered Omar.

Skip threw his arm around me like I was his long-lost pal. He stuck the microphone in my face.

"How did you know the answer, Joe?" he asked. "Are you a big fan of Stephen King?"

"Hah!" Kevin blurted. "Yeah, Joe has read every one of his books. He's a literary connoisseur!"

"I just saw him on TV at a Red Sox game," I told Skip.

"Congratulations," Skip said, shaking my hand.

It was down to two teams. In the Treasure Hunt Round, it would be the Baseball Geeks versus the obnoxious Little League Champs.

Omar, Kev, and I looked up toward the upper deck. In the first row, the Little League Champs stared down at us. Muscles was flexing his right bicep. The Lip tried to intimidate us with an exaggerated sneer. And Star pointed at us with his left hand while choking his neck with his right.

Omar put his arms around Kevin and me. He looked into the camera.

"The Baseball Geeks," he told America, "are about to kick some Little League butt!"

Chapter 4

PURSUING THE TREASURE

The show's producers treated us, including our dads, to an awesome dinner at No Name Restaurant on Fish Pier. But then it was back to Fenway Park for a dark and spooky adventure. The director took us Geeks and the Little League Champs to the upper deck. He lined us up against the fence. *Don't look down*, I told myself, but I couldn't help it. If I sat on the top of that fence and accidentally fell back, my brains would splatter on the sidewalk. A chill ran up my spine.

Skip Waybak was *trying* to make us scared. He introduced us to Hector, a grizzled man who worked on the Fenway Park cleaning crew. Hector had a look of fright in his eyes.

"I've heard ghosts," the man said. And he was serious. "When I've worked the night shift here, I've heard them."

"What exactly do you hear?" Skip prodded.

"A whole lot of racket," Hector said. "They slam doors. They turn faucets on and off when I clean the restrooms at night. I hear their footsteps. I call out: 'Anybody there? Anybody there?' And no one responds. And then I hear the sounds again."

"I brought Hector here to warn you," Skip said. "It is well documented that spirits haunt this hundred-year-old ballpark when the fans have gone home. So as you start your Treasure Hunt, beware. And be careful."

Omar leaned toward me.

"He's just trying to scare us," he whispered.

"Yeah, well, he's doing a pretty good job," I responded.

Skip explained the rules of the Treasure Hunt Round. Like before, each team would get a guide. After we answered an initial riddle, the guide would hand us our first Treasure Hunt clue. That clue would take us to another clue, which would take us to another clue. If we found one more clue after that, it would take us to our treasure.

Yorgis was our guide. A giant of a young man from some faraway country, Yorgis had white spiked hair and a grim expression. He was a night watchman at Fenway, and I'm sure they chose him as our guide in order to jack up the creepiness factor.

"He's like six-foot-ten, easy," Omar whispered to me.

Meanwhile, the Champs got Kayla as their guide. Kayla, who gave tours of Fenway Park to fans for a living, was young, pretty, and bubbly.

"If any of you guys get scared, just stay close to me," she told Muscles, Star, and the Lip. "I've got an extra-strong flashlight!"

Before we began, Skip gathered us together with our opponents. We had to stand right next to the Champs, forcing me to smell Star's bad breath and hear the Lip's gum chewing.

"First, guys," Skip said, "it's chilly out tonight, so we have jackets for you."

Bernie, the director, handed our foes dark-blue jackets that said "Little League Champs" in red letters. Our jackets, which were red with dark-blue letters, said "The Baseball Geeks."

Skip and Bernie were trying to intensify the rivalry. When we put on our Geeks jackets, the camera caught Muscles and Star snickering.

"I see that you're laughing," Skip asked Star. "How come?"

"Ah, nothin'," Star said, flipping back his long hair. "It's just . . . I'm not sure why they're here, that's all."

I could see that Kevin was getting steamed. He's the most emotional of us Geeks—and the most competitive.

"They're here because they're famous," Skip said.

"Yeah, but so what?" Muscles said. "We're here because we're the top three players on the greatest team in the world."

"Do you guys even *play* baseball," the Lip asked us with a sneer.

"Yeah, we play baseball, pal!" Kevin snapped.

"Oh, yeah?" the Lip shot back. "What's your OPS?"

"My OPS?" Kevin said.

OPS is a complicated baseball statistic. It's the sum of your on-base percentage and slugging percentage.

"Nobody keeps track of OPS in Little League," Kevin said.

"Well I did, and mine was 1.465," the Lip boasted. "What was your batting average?"

"Pretty darn good!" Kevin said.

"Oh yeah?" replied the Lip.

Bernie and Skip were loving this. It was good TV.

"Yeah," Kevin said, ".355."

"Oh really," the Lip shot back. "Mine was .618."

"Well . . . what do you want?" Kevin replied. "A cookie?"

"Not if *you* made it," the Lip said.

Sensing that Kevin was about to knock the sneer right off the Lip's face, Skip stepped between them.

"Okay, okay!" Skip said, eyeing the camera. "It looks like we've got a little rivalry brewing. Stay tuned, folks, as the Geeks and the Champs square off in what will undoubtedly be a hotly contested Treasure Hunt Round."

Kevin, Omar, and I huddled together, while the Champs walked toward Kayla. A cameraman was assigned to each group (we got Stan again), while our dads looked down on us from a skybox.

"You need to calm down, Kev," I said.

"We gotta kick their pompous butts," he said, for everyone to hear.

"You got a big mouth!" Muscles shouted.

"Yeah," Kevin retorted. "Well, you've got a small brain!"

"My IQ is 120," Muscles replied.

"Out of what?" Omar quipped. "A thousand?"

"We'll *see* who's smarter," Star retorted.

After all the trash talk, we decided to bear down and get crackin'. Yorgis handed each of us a flashlight. He then pulled out a card and read us a riddle. He talked in a super-deep voice without emotion.

"What is the minimum amount of pitches," he intoned, "that can be thrown in a complete nine-inning Major League Baseball game?"

"Well," I said. "If every batter on both teams lined out to the second baseman on the first pitch . . ."

"Or the shortstop," Kevin added.

"Or whomever," I said, "then that would be six total pitches per inning. After eight innings, that would be forty-eight pitches."

"Then what about the ninth inning?" Kevin asked.

"That's easy," Omar said. "The visiting team goes down on three pitches. That brings us up to fifty-one pitches."

"And then," Kevin said, "David 'Big Papi' Ortiz leads off the bottom of the ninth with a walk-off homer!"

"That's pitch number fifty-two," I said.

"And that's our answer," Omar said. "Fifty-two. Is that right, Yorgis?"

"Yes," he said.

Yorgis was no Laverne. We got no touchdown dance, hug, high-five—nothin'.

"This guy's like Frankenstein's boring cousin," Kevin whispered to me.

The Champs finished the question just as quickly. While Kayla gave them their first Treasure Hunt clue, Yorgis did the same for us. He handed us a card that seemed to read:

Fenway Challenge Clue:
406 = 502

We stared blankly at the card.

"How much help are you going to be to us?" Kevin asked Yorgis.

"Not much," he replied, prompting Kevin to roll his eyes.

I focused the flashlight more sharply on the card.

"Wait," I said. "There's a dot before the '406.' It says '.406.'"

"Like a batting average," Omar said.

"Like *Ted Williams'* batting average!" Kevin said. "He's the last major-league player to bat .400, and I believe he hit .406. Is that right, Yorgis?"

"Yes," Yorgis said.

Entering the last day of the 1941 season, Williams was batting an even .400. His manager suggested that he take the last day off to ensure that his average would remain .400—and not drop below that mark. But Williams, who would fly combat planes for the Marines during the Korean War, wasn't the type to take the easy way out. He played that final day, facing the Philadelphia A's in both games of a doubleheader. He cracked four singles, a double, and a homer and finished the season at .406. As Kevin said, no one has batted .400 since.

"So how can .406 equal 502?" I asked.

"Maybe .406 represents Ted Williams himself," Kevin said.

Yorgis nodded.

"Okay, we got a nod," Kevin said. "Now what can 502 represent in baseball? And not 502 home runs, because I know Williams hit more than that."

"What's the furthest he hit a homer?" Omar said. "Five hundred and two feet?"

Yorgis nodded again. Good job, Kev and Omar!

"Follow me," Yorgis bellowed.

The big guy led us to the dark concourse—the walkway between the seating area and the food stands. Yorgis was leading us toward the seat where the Splendid Splinter's 502-foot home run landed. But first, he stopped to use the men's room.

"Wait here," he said.

Kevin, Omar, and I stood by ourselves in silence. I kept thinking about the stories that Hector had told us. About the phantom noises. Slamming doors. Faucets. Footsteps.... Suddenly, I heard a crash!

"What's that?!" I blurted.

"It's the toilet seat," Omar said as Stan the cameraman burst into laughter. "Yorgis should be out any second."

Okay, it was just the toilet. But I couldn't stop my heart from racing. Yorgis walked us all the way to the right-center-field seats.

"The seat is now red," Yorgis said. "Go get your clue."

The seat where Williams hit the ball—Section 42, Row 37, Seat 21—

was painted red by the Red Sox. It was the sole red seat in a sea of green.

"Joey," Stan the cameraman said, "you go."

The cameraman was playing director. He wanted me to go because, apparently, I was the biggest scaredy cat. But I bravely walked down to Seat 21, where an envelope was wedged between the slats. I opened it and shone a light on the card inside.

"What does it say?" Omar shouted from above.

"Hot dog, 44!" I yelled back.

From the third base seats I heard, from the Lip, "*You're* a hot dog!"

"Really funny!" Kevin shouted to the Lip. "I almost laughed!"

What the Lip didn't realize is that he helped us get the answer. Our first thought would have been to check out the hot dog stands, especially the one closest to Section 44. But in baseball, a "hot dog" refers to a certain type of player. A hot dog is a show-off. He has a big ego. He thinks he's better than everyone else, and he says so.

"Reggie Jackson!" Kevin declared. "He was baseball's biggest hot dog in the 1970s.

"*And*," Omar added, "he wore No. 44!"

Stan the cameraman turned to me.

"How do you guys *know* all this?" he asked me.

I shrugged.

"We just do," I said. "In fact, I remember someone saying about Jackson: 'There isn't enough mustard to cover that hot dog.'"

Yorgis, with a grunt, confirmed that Reggie was our man. But where was the clue?

"Maybe in right field," Kevin said. "That's were Reggie played."

Jackson never played for the Red Sox, but he often visited Fenway Park as a star slugger for the Oakland A's and New York Yankees. My dad told me about a game in Fenway in 1976. The Yankees' fiery manager, Billy Martin, thought Reggie wasn't hustling in right field. So he pulled him out of the game. The two started yelling at each other in the dugout. Martin was so angry, he nearly threw a punch. That wouldn't have been surprising. Years earlier, Martin had punched out a marshmallow salesman.

Anyway, Yorgis let us run around right field looking for a clue. It was pretty cool to play on the same grass that Babe

Ruth had roamed ninety years earlier. I pointed my flashlight into the sky, pretending that a fly ball was headed my way. But as for a clue, we looked and looked but couldn't find it.

"Where else would Reggie Jackson be?" Omar shouted from right-center field.

Kevin and I looked at each other. The answer was obvious. The visitor's dugout—the same place where Billy Martin nearly punched him out. We ran into the dugout and looked on the long benches, but didn't find a clue.

"Look!" Omar said.

In the corner of the dugout was a stack of twelve cubby-holes, with a dark helmet in each one. When we pulled them out, they all seemed to be Red Sox helmets—except for the very last one.

"Yankees!" I exclaimed. "And it says No. 44 on the back."

Sure enough, an envelope was glued to the inside of the helmet. I ripped it off, opened it, and read the next clue as Omar shined a flashlight on the card.

Like gnats.

"Man, these clues get shorter and shorter," Omar complained.

Just then, we heard some cheering from the upper deck. The Champs had just found their second clue also.

"You need to hurry up," advised Yorgis, who stood outside the dugout with a bat. He took some practice cuts with a big left-handed swing.

"Hey, Joe," Omar asked. "How far do you think Yorgis could hit a baseball?"

Kevin was annoyed.

"What does that have to do with gnats?" he asked.

"Nothing," Omar replied. "But the guy's so huge, and he's left-handed, so he could easily reach the fences in right."

"Anybody could homer to right field," Kevin said. "It's only 302 feet to Pesky's Pole. Now, let's figure out this gnat situation."

The three of us looked at each other. Gnats. Pesky. Gnats are pesky. I shone a flashlight on Yorgis, who actually grinned. He had successfully given us a clue without saying a word.

"Pesky's Pole!" the three of us exclaimed in unison.

Back in the 1950s, the right-field foul pole was named after longtime Red Sox infielder Johnny Pesky. According to legend, he had a knack for hitting home runs off that pole—which is listed at

302 feet from home plate. Ever since, it has been known as Pesky's Pole, which many fans have signed with markers.

Chugging across the field, we headed toward the right-field corner. The fence out there is short—only about my height—and the bottom of the pole starts at the top of the fence.

"Your clue," Yorgis said, "is written on the pole—way up high."

He then reached over the railing, into the stands, and pulled out an aluminum ladder. He leaned it against the pole.

"Who is brave?" he asked us.

"I'm afraid of heights," I said, chickening out.

"I'm afraid of cracking my skull open," Kevin said.

"I'll do it," Omar offered. "You guys bailed me out at Wrigley Field. I owe ya."

The Big O began his ascent. When he got to a point where the signatures stopped, he focused on some words.

"I got it," Omar said, and he climbed down the ladder.

"What did it say?" I asked anxiously.

"It said, 'Final clue: In the belly of the beast.'"

"In the belly of the *Monster*!" Kevin blurted, pointing to left field. "The *Green* Monster!"

I *knew* that's where the Treasure Hunt would end! But how would we get in there? There was only one entrance, the door along the base of the wall, but it was always kept locked.

"How do we get in there?" I asked Yorgis.

"Check your pockets," he replied.

We each dug our hands into the pockets of our Baseball Geeks jackets.

Nothing. Then I realized that small pockets were sewn into the left sleeves. I unzipped mine and—voila!—pulled out a key.

"You better hurry," Yorgis said. "The other team found their key, too."

Looking into the stands behind first base, we saw the Champs scrambling like madmen down the steps. They, too, were headed toward the Green Monster!

"Holy cannoli!" Kevin screamed. "Let's go!"

Like Coco Crisp chasing a fly ball, we sprinted across the outfield grass. We had a big head start on the Champs, but whoa Nellie, those kids were fast! As we reached left field, they were already in center.

"Get your key ready!" Omar yelled.

"I got it!" I cried.

I beelined toward the door and jammed the key into the lock as fast as I could.

"Hurry up!" Kevin screamed. "They're coming!"

I twisted the handle, and we barged through the doorway. As the Champs approached the warning track, Kevin slammed the door, then bolted it shut. That way, not even their key could get them in.

"Open up!" one of the Champs demanded.

"Open this door," another shouted, "you little . . ."

"The only thing little are your brains!" yelled an out-of-breath Kevin.

The three of us broke into grins and laughs, then focused on finding our remaining clue. The room was pitch-black, lit only by our flashlights.

"This place is creepy," I said. "Like an old attic."

The ceiling was slanted, with concrete beams. Like the Pesky Pole, words were scrawled all over the walls. Most noticeably, the room was loaded with number signs. If the Red Sox scored two runs in the first inning, a worker would put a "2" sign in the first-inning window.

We heard another knock. Kevin huffed.

"I told you an hour ago to suck eggs!" Kev shouted.

"It's Stan," the voice said, "the cameraman."

"Oh," Kevin said.

We let Stan in. After he turned his camera on, he spoke into a microphone.

"I'm here to inform you," he told us, "that you have exactly two minutes to find your Treasure Hunt prize."

"And if we don't—what?" Kevin snapped back. "The room will blow up?"

"If you don't find it in two minutes," the cameraman replied, "you don't get your prize. You're down to a minute and fifty seconds."

The room was pretty sparse except for the green number signs, but they were laying everywhere. It made sense that there were so many. If each team scored one run in every inning, that's eighteen "1s" that they would have to hang. So they had to have enough number signs for every possible situation.

The treasure had to be under the number signs. At first, we respectfully lifted the signs. But now we were flinging them like playing cards.

"Thirty seconds!" the cameraman warned.

Stuck in the far corner of the room, on the damp and dusty floor, was a hefty stack of number signs. I ran over there and whacked the stack with my hand. As the signs scattered on the floor, I saw it: a large, white envelope, trimmed in gold.

"I got it!" I screamed.

Omar, Kev, and the cameraman ran over. Skip opened the door and barged in.

"Are you sure?" Omar asked me.

"Yes," I said, shining my light on the envelope. "It says 'The Treasure' right on it."

"Way to go, Geeks!" Skip said, shaking our hands. "How do you feel?"

"Awesome!" Kevin said.

"I feel like a kid at Christmas," Omar said, "in the bowels of Fenway Park."

"Hah!" laughed Skip. "You're anxious to see what's in the envelope, aren't yah?"

We nodded eagerly.

"Open it up," Skip said to me.

I must say, I was pretty darn excited. The back of the envelope was sealed with a gold sticker. I looked at Omar and Kevin, whose faces beamed in anticipation.

"This is like the Oscars," Skip said, "only you're the winners."

I peeled off the gold sticker and pulled out a card. It was fancy, like a special invitation.

"Read it, Kevin," Skip said.

"Congratulations to the winners of the Fenway Park Challenge," I read aloud. "You are invited to play in this year's Fenway Fantasy Game, right here at Fenway Park, on Father's Day. Your opponents will be Red Sox Legends, including Hall of Famers Jim Rice and Carlton Fisk. It's a fantasy come true."

"Awesome," Kevin said, smiling.

"Very cool," Omar added.

"Way to go, guys!" Skip said. "So you'll come back for Father's Day? Bring your dads?"

"Uhmm . . . ," said a hesitant Omar.

"We'll pay all the expenses," Skip added with a laugh.

"Then yeah," Omar confirmed. "I'm sure we will."

And we did.

Chapter 5

A FENWAY FANTASY

~~~~~~~~~~~~~~~~~~~~~~~~~~~~~~~~~~

Omar, Kevin, and I sat disappointingly in the Red Sox dugout. After five innings of the six-inning Fenway Fantasy Game, we had yet to play.

Don't get me wrong: it had been a phenomenal Father's Day weekend. My whole family—dad, mom, and fourteen-year-old brother Dan—came this time. It was another beautiful, sunshiny day. And before the game, us Geeks got to put on real Red Sox uniforms in the Red Sox locker room. I chose No. 15 for

Dustin Pedroia, Boston's five-foot-eight All-Star second baseman. Kev selected No. 5 in honor of the great Red Sox shortstop Nomar Garciaparra.

"His nickname was Nomah," Omar had said. "So you should call me Omah."

"Omah" thought about choosing No. 12 for Pumpsie Green, Boston's first African-American player. But instead he went with No. 27, Carlton Fisk's number.

"Maybe I'll hit one off the left-field foul pole," Omar had said.

Now, we wondered if we were even going to play. We were just three of twenty players on our Red Sox Fantasy team. All the others were rich men— doctors, lawyers, etc.—who paid $10,000 apiece to be on this team. For that money, each expected to play at least a couple innings. They paid to face the Red Sox Legends team, which included such greats as Fisk, slugger Fred Lynn, and Hall of Fame pitcher Dennis Eckersley.

"But they've *got* to play us in the last inning," Kevin said, meaning the sixth. "*Sports Jr.* is here to film us."

Finally, Skip McCloskey, our manager for the day, walked up to us with his lineup card. The elderly gentleman used to be a Red Sox coach in the 1970s.

"Baseball Geeks!" he barked. "You're going in next inning. Ovozi, right field. Kernacki, second base."

"Yes!" Kevin exclaimed.

"Evers, left field," Skip said, and then he walked away.

I suddenly got all jittery. My hands and feet began to shake. When the last out of the fifth inning was recorded, I ran out to left field. I looked into the stands, where several thousand people cheered—mostly for us kids. My parents and even my brother gave us a standing ovation. TV cameras were there, too. We would be on the local news and, of course, *Sports Jr.*

"And the new left fielder," boomed the public address announcer, "Joe Evers."

I just hope they don't hit it to me, I kept telling myself.

Entering the sixth, the score was tied at 5–5. This looked like it would be an easy inning, as our pitcher retired the first two Legends batters—on a strikeout and a grounder to first. But the next two hitters were Lynn and Rice. In 1975, these two Red Sox rookies were called the "Gold Dust Twins." That year, center fielder Lynn became the first rookie to ever be named league MVP.

And now he ripped a screaming liner to right for a two-out single.

That brought up Rice. As the American League MVP in 1978, Rice blasted forty-six home runs. The right-handed slugger especially loved hitting at Fenway, where he batted .320 for his career. Our shortstop, Dr. Jones, turned and looked at me.

"Back up," he told me. "And get ready."

Sure enough, Rice took a mighty rip and launched a rocket to left field— over my head. As I ran back toward the warning track, I realized the ball was going to hit near the top of the Green Monster. Wisely, I retreated away from the wall and caught the ball off the ricochet. I immediately turned and fired a strike to second base. Rice was trying to stretch the hit into a double. But my throw landed in the glove of Kevin, who applied the tag on the sliding Hall of Famer for the inning's third out.

"You're outta there!" the umpire declared.

"Ted Williams couldn't have played that any better!" blared the P.A. announcer.

In the dugout, my wealthy teammates gave me high-fives and patted me on the head.

"You kept us in the game, son!" Skip said. "Freddy Lynn was about to score on the play."

I was the eighth scheduled hitter in the bottom of the sixth, so I definitely wouldn't bat. But Kevin would lead off, and Omar would be the third batter.

"Get us started, Kev!" Omar encouraged.

Kevin stood in against Eckersley, who was known for his great control. But with Kevin only four-foot-ten—and batting out of a crouch, Eck had a hard time throwing strikes. Kevin walked on a 3–2 pitch, then ran to first base. Eckersley laughed.

"His strike zone is the size of a postage stamp!" Eck said.

In Little League, Kevin steals bases like Bonnie and Clyde robbed banks. Sure enough, he ran on the first pitch. Carlton Fisk's throw was off-target, giving Kevin a stolen base. He thrust up his arms in victory.

"Way to go, Kev!" his dad shouted from the stands.

Eckersley struck out the next batter, bringing up Omar. And that's when things got interesting.

In the dugout, some of the men started muttering about Fisk and Eckersley and Kirk Gibson. I started piecing the details together. Fisk's home run in 1975 was one of the greatest in World Series history. And here was Omar, wearing Fisk's number and standing two feet away from the Series hero. But the irony didn't end there. After his years with the Red Sox, Eckersley pitched for Oakland in the 1988 World Series. In Game 1, he faced Los Angeles Dodgers slugger Kirk Gibson. Gibby was so injured that he had begun the game in street clothes. He limped to the batter's box. And then he belted a game-winning homer. It, too, was one of the greatest hits in World Series history.

So, with Eckersley ready to throw to catcher Fisk, Omar stood at home plate, ready to play the role of Kirk Gibson. Omar is a tall kid with a huge left-handed swing. When he swung and missed on Eck's first pitch, the crowd gasped.

"What a swing!" Dr. Jones marveled. "And the wind is blowing out."

"If this kid connects...," Skip mused.

Omar worked the count to 3–1. Eckersley tugged at his belt. He checked Kevin at second base. Then he wound, kicked, and delivered. With a mighty rip, Omar launched a towering fly ball down the right-field line. My teammates and I rushed to the steps of the dugout.

"That's got a chance!" Skip marveled.

In the catcher's box, Fisk stood up and flipped off his mask. Eckersley cocked his head toward the sky, wondering if it would be 1988 all over again. And there was Omar, not running but instead watching the flight of the ball. As the ball descended, it was clear that it had the distance. But would it stay fair?

Like Carlton Fisk, Omar waved his arms toward fair territory, trying to

"wave" the ball fair. And then: BANG!
Right off the Pesky Pole!

Omar jumped to the heavens as he
trotted around the bases with his walk-
off home run. My teammates and I ran
onto the field. Kevin dove head-first
into home plate, just for the fun of it.
The fans, who were going wild, began
chanting "O-mar! O-mar!" The Big O's
mom and dad jumped over the rail and
ran to greet their son. Kevin and I were
the first to mob Omar as he reached the
plate.

"Omar Ovozi," the P.A. announcer
boomed, "has just become the youngest
player ever to hit a home run at Fenway
Park!"

"Congratulations," Fisk said to Omar,
shaking his hand. "I couldn't have done
it better myself!"

Out in the stands, Bernie Rohrbacher kissed his wife, Laverne, and slapped skin with Skip Wayback. Bernie was thrilled because all of the drama had been captured on film and would air on *Sports Jr.* And that, he was certain, would make for "good TV."

Read each title in **The Baseball Geeks Adventures**

A HALL Lot of Trouble at Cooperstown
The Baseball Geeks Adventures Book 1

When Joe, Kevin, and Omar take a trip to Cooperstown to save Kevin's dad, will the boys be able save themselves from the "trouble" they get into?

ISBN: 978-1-62285-118-8

Foul Ball Frame-up at Wrigley Field
The Baseball Geeks Adventures Book 2

After Omar is "framed" for an incident that was out of his hands, can Joe and Kevin save their friend from becoming one of the biggest curses in history?

ISBN: 978-1-62285-123-2

The Treasure Hunt Stunt at Fenway Park
The Baseball Geeks Adventures Book 3

Joe, Kevin, and Omar want a shot at the Treasure Hunt Round. But can the Geeks beat the Little League Champs before they "stunt" the Geeks' chances of winning it all?

ISBN: 978-1-62285-128-7

Bossing the Bronx Bombers at Yankee Stadium
The Baseball Geeks Adventures Book 4

When the Geeks are invited to watch a game from a luxury suite, Joe, Kevin, and Omar find themselves in a bad situation when they start making some "bossy" calls.

ISBN: 978-1-62285-133-1